*Thanks to Daphne Cox for
her assistance and support.*

*The recipes in this book are
from the kitchen of Daphne Cox.*

Library of Congress Cataloging-in-Publication Data Available

2   4   6   8   10   9   7   5   3   1

Published by Sterling Publishing Co., Inc.
387 Park Avenue South, New York, NY 10016
Originally published in 1997 by Viking Press
Text copyright © 2004 by Ella Grier
Illustration copyright © 2004 by John Ward
Distributed in Canada by Sterling Publishing
c/o Canadian Manda Group, One Atlantic Avenue, Suite 105
Toronto, Ontario, Canada M6K 3E7
Distributed in Great Britain and Europe by Chris Lloyd at Orca Book
Services, Stanley House, Fleets Lane, Poole BH15 3AJ, England
Distributed in Australia by Capricorn Link (Australia) Pty. Ltd.
P.O. Box 704, Windsor, NSW 2756, Australia

Sterling ISBN 1-4027-1939-6

SEVEN DAYS OF
KWANZAA

A Holiday Step Book

by Ella Grier
pictures by John Ward

Sterling Publishing Co., Inc.
New York

FIRST DAY

December 26, first day of Kwanzaa
Principle: Umoja (Unity)
Symbol: Mazao (Straw basket of fruit)

Call your father!
Call your mother!
Call your sister!
Call your brother!

It's Kwanzaa time. Family time.
It's Kwanzaa time. Family time.

African-American people pulling
together—Harambee.
Trying to make things better.
Seven days and seven nights,
Seven candles we will light.
Seven candles we will light.

—a Kwanzaa song

SECOND DAY

December 27, second day of Kwanzaa
Principle: Kujichagulia (Self-determination)
Symbol: Mkeka (Straw mat)

Relatives come to visit.
The cousins say, *"Harambee!"*
We make *mkeka* mats.
It's fun working together.

It's Kwanzaa time. Family time.
It's Kwanzaa time. Family time.

THIRD DAY

December 28, third day of Kwanzaa
Principle: Ujima (Working together)
Symbol: Kinara (Wooden candleholder)

We sweep the yard.
We paint the gate.
Everything looks better.

We are pulling together.
We are pulling together.
We are pulling together.
Oh yes we are.

FOURTH DAY

December 29, fourth day of Kwanzaa
Principle: Ujamaa (Sharing profit)
Symbol: Muhindi (Ears of corn)

We go to Malcolm's Market.
Malcolm asks, *"Habari gani*–What's the news?"
We say, *"Ujamaa!"*
Mama buys corn and sweet potatoes.

> *One potato, two potato,*
> *Three potato, sweet!*
> *Four potato, five potato,*
> *Six potato, eat!*

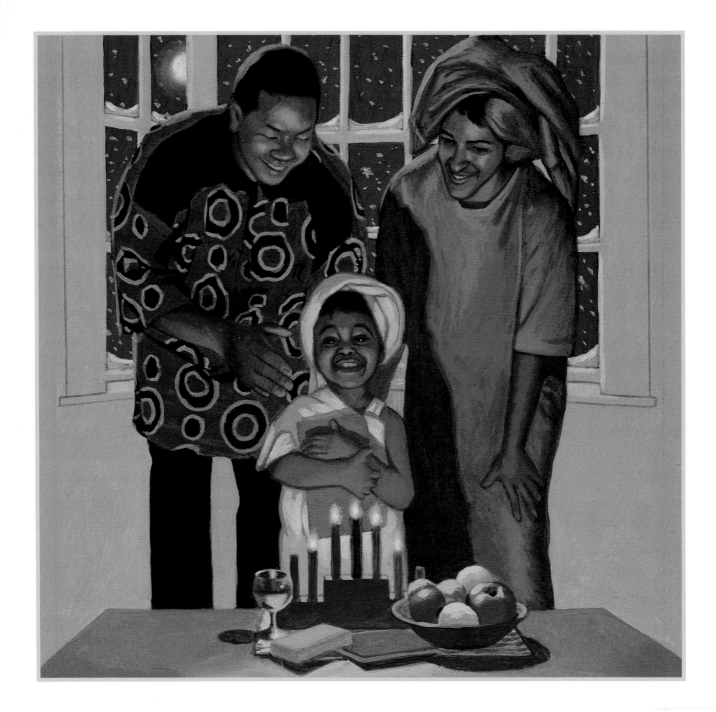

FIFTH DAY

December 30, fifth day of Kwanzaa
Principle: Nia (Purpose)
Symbol: Zawadi (Handmade gift or book)

Here's how we light the candles.
First the black, next a red,
then a green, then another red,
and then another green.

This little light of mine —
I'm gonna let it shine.
This little light of mine —
I'm gonna let it shine.
Let it shine. Let it shine.
Let it shine.

SIXTH DAY

December 31, sixth day of Kwanzaa
Principle: Kuumba (Creativity)
Symbol: Kikombe Cha Umoja (Unity cup)

Everyone plays "I've Got the Spirit!"
Grandma beats a drum.
Papa claps.
Everyone dances to the rhythm.

Leader: *I've got the spirit!*
All: *Hey, hey!*
Leader: *I've got the spirit!*
All: *Ashé, ashé!*
Leader: *I've got the spirit!*
All: *Hey, hey!*
Leader: *I've got Kuumba!*
All: *Ashé, ashé!*

We dance and sing until we are tired out.

SEVENTH DAY

January 1, seventh day of Kwanzaa
Principle: Imani (Faith)
Symbol: Mishumaa Saba (Seven candles)

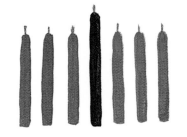

We light all seven candles.
Grandpa tells a story of how our people
came from Africa long ago. He says,
"May we all live by the *Nguzo Saba,*
the seven principles of Kwanzaa."

Keep the faith.
That's the thing to do.
Believe in yourself
And your family, too.

Keep Imani in your heart.
Keep Imani in your soul.
Imani is more precious
Than diamonds or gold.